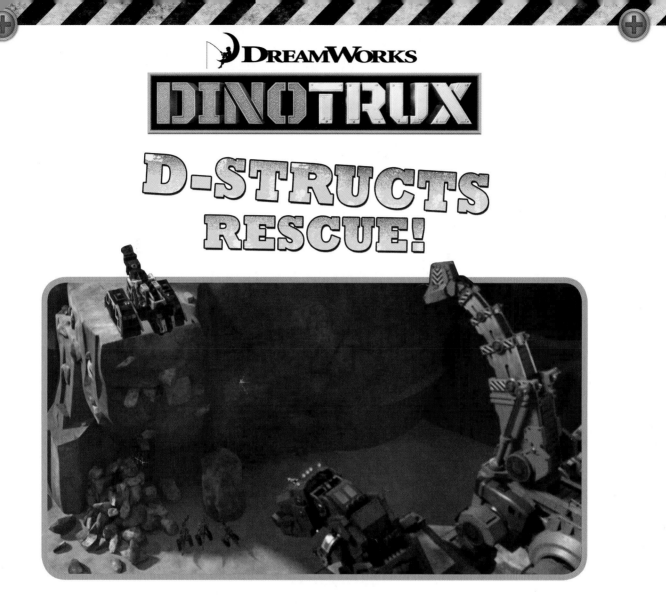

DreamWorks
DINOTRUX
D-STRUCTS RESCUE!

Adapted by Elizabeth Milton

LITTLE, BROWN & COMPANY
LB kids

Little, Brown and Company

Hachette Book Group
1290 Avenue of the Americas, New York, NY 10104
Visit us at lb-kids.com

LB kids is an imprint of Little, Brown and Company.
The LB kids name and logo are trademarks of Hachette Book Group, Inc.

The publisher is not responsible for websites (or their content) that are not owned by the publisher.

First Edition: September 2016

Library of Congress Control Number: 2016938031

ISBN 978-0-316-26087-9

10 9 8 7 6 5 4 3 2 1

CW

Printed in the United States of America

"**W**hat's taking so long?" D-Structs's voice boomed in the cave. Skrap-It twitched. The Reptools had taken D-Structs's old wrecking-ball tail to keep him from destroying their ravine, and Skrap-It was scrambling to weld a new one out of scrap metal.

"Just one last bolt and…all done!" Skrap-It said. "So, does the mighty D-Structs approve?"

D-Structs glared and swung his new tail at Skrap-It. The vine attaching the wrecking ball snapped, and it hit Skrap-It and slammed into the cave wall.

"I don't need a wrecking ball to do *my* wrecking," D-Structs sneered. "I'm going to take apart the first Dinotrux I see!"

"You're right. You're scary enough without it," Skrap-It said weakly.

Meanwhile, the Dinotrux were smashing rocks for the new rock depot. Ty Rux rammed his tail into a granite rock wall, breaking it into pieces. "Let's see someone smash more rocks than *that*," Ty dared the gang.

Skya hooked her crane tongue into a quartz wall and tugged. "Wait for it…" she said, and blew a puff of air. Dozens of boulders crashed to the ground! "Boom! Did it!"

Garby was keeping track. "The gang's got quartz, marble, granite, and sandstone," he told Waldo and Click-Clack. "There's still a soft rock we haven't gotten yet, and I know where to find a whole valley full of it!"

Ty, Revvit, Skya, Dozer, and Ton-Ton crossed the crater to get to the valley, but stopped in their tracks when they saw D-structs!

"That dude's not gonna take *all* of us on at once," Ton-Ton said.

"Yeah, especially not without his ol' ball and chain," Dozer said.

Ty warned them that even without a tail, D-Structs was still trouble.

Ty was right. D-Structs bolted at the group and flipped over Ton-Ton! Then he began to charge at Ty.

"I don't want to fight you," Ty said.

"Too bad, because *I* want to fight *you*!" D-Structs growled.

That's when Revvit noticed that the ground under D-Structs's tread was cracking. "Ty, look out! The rock in this valley is very soft, remember?"

Ty quickly rolled backward. "D-Structs, you really don't want to be standing there," he warned.

"Do you really think he's going to fall for that?" Skrap-It yelled, thinking they were trying to fool D-Structs.

D-Structs revved his engine, and the ground collapsed beneath his treads! He and Skrap-It fell out of sight. They landed on a small ledge in the canyon below. When the dust settled, Ty and the gang peered over the edge of what was now a cliff.

"I know D-Structs wanted to take us down, but I don't think he meant like that!" said Dozer.

Just then, at the bottom of the canyon, a pack of Scraptors screeched.

"Just try and scrap me," D-Structs yelled at the Scraptors, but they were already trying to climb up to the ledge.

"We gotta do something!" said Ty.

"Yeah, leave him there and let him get what he deserves," Dozer said. "He's the bad guy."

"He's still a Dinotrux," Ty said.

"But it's not safe to tow him up from here with all this soft rock under our treads," Skya replied.

"Maybe we can get to the other side of the cliff and build something to get him up!" Ton-Ton said.

Dozer couldn't believe that Ton-Ton wanted to help D-Structs...especially after D-Structs had just flipped him over!

Ty knew they had to help. "Dozer, *we're* not gonna change the kind of Trux we are just because of the kind of Trux *D-Structs* is. So are you in or not?"

Dozer nodded. "Fine, but I'm not gonna like it."

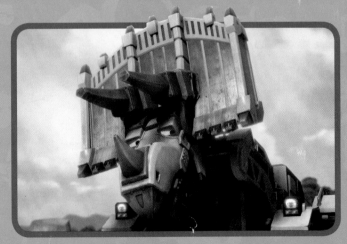

Revvit had a plan. "All we need to do is bridge the gap between the edge of this cliff and the ledge on which D-Structs is stranded," he explained.

He etched a blueprint on a rock.

"A ramp bridge! *Awwwesome,*" said Ton-Ton.

Dozer and Ty cut down trees to use as supports. Skya lowered the tree trunks into the canyon, and Ty pounded them into the ground with his wrecking ball.

Caw! Caw! A Scrapadactyl flock circled overhead. There was no time to lose!

Revvit measured the stones for the ramp, Dozer dozed them, and Ton-Ton hauled them. All the while, D-Structs was hurling boulders at them!

"I'm getting the feeling this guy doesn't want to be saved," Dozer said.

Even so, the gang kept working. When the supports were ready, it was time to start sliding the stone ramp into place.

When the ramp bridge was ready, Skrap-It didn't hesitate to run across it! "You know, I've always been a big fan of you Trux!" he said gratefully.

The Scraptors had almost reached D-Structs on the ledge, but he wouldn't budge.

"You coming or not? Last chance!" Ty told him.

Just as the Scraptors leapt onto the ledge, D-Structs raced to safety.

"Skya, now!" Ty said.

Skya hooked the bridge with her crane tongue and gave a quick tug.

"You're gonna have to pull harder than that!" Ton-Ton told her.

"Wait for it…" Skya said. Then she blew on the bridge, and it fell into the canyon below. Without the bridge, the Scraptors couldn't reach the Dinotrux!

Seeing that D-Structs and Skrap-It were safe, the Scrapadactyls flew away.

"You're welcome?" Ty hinted to D-Structs.

D-Structs ignored Ty and barreled past the Trux, knocking them out of his path.

"Do you believe that T-Trux? Not even a thank you!" said Dozer.

Following D-Structs into the woods, Skrap-It spotted a pile of scrap metal and had an idea. "You'll never have to be saved by those Trux ever again," Skrap-It promised as he shared his plan. "Does the mighty D-Structs approve?"

"You actually did something right for a change," D-Structs said. "Now, get to work!"

Soon after, Ty and the gang were back at the rock depot, competing to see who could stack their rock piles the highest. They heard a noise that sounded like a saw. It was D-Structs! Skrap-It had used the scrap metal to make a buzz-saw tail.

"I never offered my appreciation to you Trux for saving me, or for taking my old tail. So allow me to say it now: thank you!" D-Structs roared angrily.

D-Structs used his tail to saw through everything in sight! Ty gathered all his strength to whack it with his wrecking ball. The buzz saw broke off and flew into the air!

"Are we done?" Ty asked. When D-Structs saw that he was without a tail *again*, he roared so loudly the ground shook. After he stormed off, Ty turned to the gang and smiled. "Well, at least we finally got that thank you he owed us!"